Sunny

Theresa MacInnis Schimmel

Illustrated by Dennis Lavorato

www.tamstales.net

To Emerson —
May you always have
love in your heart! ♡

Theresa MacInnes Schimmel

Dedicated to all foster parents and foster children,
especially Beth and Mark, and Nick and Derek (now adopted).

Mandy woke up all excited. Today was the day that Mama Rose had promised that they would go visit the puppies. She stretched her arms and swung out of bed. She put her feet into her fuzzy green slippers, and went down the stairs.

Mama Rose was in the kitchen fixing breakfast. Mandy could smell French toast with cinnamon, her favorite. "Mornin', honey." Mama Rose bent down and gave Mandy a soft kiss. "Are you hungry?" Mandy nodded, and sat down at the kitchen table. The kitchen curtains blew in from the gentle morning breeze outside. It seemed so quiet. Mandy's old neighborhood was full of morning noises: the garbage truck going by, the people in the streets below, the *"Honk"* of cars and *"Eeee"* of ambulance or police sirens. No longer did she hear the cries of her baby brother or the chattering of her little sister.

Mama Rose set the French toast and a glass of milk in front of Mandy. She poured herself another cup of coffee and sat down at the table. "You haven't forgotten where we're going today, have you, Mandy?" Mandy shook her head as she poured the thick brown syrup on her plate. She liked the way Mama Rose spoke so soft to her and always smiled so nice. "Mr. Johnson says we can come on over anytime today. Sounds like that stray dog that found its way into his barn had quite a litter last week. Guess how many puppies she had?"

Mandy found her voice and said, "I don't know, four?"

"Would you believe nine? Saints preserve us, that's a parcel! How about we go on over there after you dress and make your bed, while I clean up the kitchen?"

"Okay."

Mandy finished her French toast, swallowed the last of her milk, and headed up the stairs to her bedroom. She had her own bedroom now, with a big soft pillow. Mandy tucked the sheets in carefully, just the way Mama Rose had taught her. In her old room, she had never made her bed, maybe because she had shared it with her sister. Every morning they dressed in a hurry to avoid waking up their baby brother in the crib next to them. Her sister and brother were in another house now. She had not seen them since she left the apartment almost a month ago.

Mandy picked out her own clothes. Mama Rose had taken her shopping and now there was a dresser full of new clothes. She put on the new blue jeans and pink striped shirt. Then she opened the top drawer, searching for the one item she needed most. She spotted the orange polka dotted headband. Rubbing the fuzzy cloth, she slipped it over her straight yellow hair. Once Mama Rose put it in the laundry bin and Mandy couldn't find it. She had cried until she saw it peeking out from the towels on top. It was all she had from home.

"Are you almost ready, Mandy? Mr. Johnson just called to find out what time we'd be over."

"I'll be right there." Mandy put on her clogs, and pulled the yellow bedspread over the pillow. She ran down the stairs, thinking about the new puppies she was about to see. She loved animals. Stray cats and dogs used to hang around the alleys next to her old apartment building. Sometimes they would even come to her when she called, especially when she had saved a table scrap for them to eat.

Mama Rose was just finishing the dishes when Mandy walked in. "Well, don't you look pretty in that new outfit! Glad you wore your clogs and jeans. You know how muddy Mr. Johnson's farmyard can be. Just got to bundle up these biscuits and jam I made for him, and we'll be on our way."

Mandy held Mama Rose's hand on the way to Mr. Johnson's. They walked along a side dirt road until reaching a big open field. There were bright yellow sunflowers in the field. Sunflowers always made Mandy smile. "Would you like to run the rest of the way, honey?"

"Can I?"

"Sure." Mama Rose let go of her hand and Mandy ran through the field. The tall yellow-green grass brushed against her jeans; the summer breeze caressed her face. She loved to run. Sometimes when her Daddy used to come to visit he would take her to the city park and she would run. Daddy said that she could run like a colt. She wished that Daddy could have come to take her that night she had to leave the apartment, but Daddy hadn't come to visit in a very long time. When she had asked her mother about him, she said he wasn't ever coming back.

As she reached the end of the field, she could see Mr. Johnson's place and she could hear Mama Rose yelling from behind her, "Wait for me!"

Mr. Johnson was out in his garden picking blueberries from his blueberry bushes. He set the basket down when he saw them coming.

"Howdy Rose. I see you brought little Mandy with you." He stepped out of his garden. "Try some of these beauties, Mandy." He opened his hand and Mandy saw big purplish blue berries. She put some in her mouth. "Sweet, huh?" Mandy nodded. "You ready to see those puppies now?" Again Mandy nodded.

The barn was old and dark. A shaft of morning sunlight came through the cracked roof. Mandy heard a yipping noise as they entered and then high pitched little whines. She followed the sound until she saw them. Furry tan balls nuzzled against their mother's nipples. They were whimpering and falling all over each other.

"Can I pick one up, Mr. Johnson?"

"Sure you can, Mandy."

Mandy scooped up one of the little puppies. Its nose was soft and wet. She pressed it up against her chest and then watched it wiggle up to her neck, where it lay soft and warm against her skin. Mandy smiled and smiled. She stayed in the barn with the puppies for most of the morning. Mama Rose helped Mr. Johnson with some of his farm chores and then came to collect her. Mandy took one last look at the puppies, took Mama Rose's hand and walked home, swinging the pail of blueberries that Mr. Johnson had given her.

Mandy visited the puppies every day. She'd watch them squirm all over, and yip. Sometimes they would toddle over to her and she would pick them up one by one. No two puppies were exactly alike. The smallest one, a soft tawny brown, sometimes had trouble finding a place to nurse. Mandy would pick her up and place her gently onto her mother's nipple.

One morning Mandy woke up hearing voices in the kitchen. She dressed quickly and ran downstairs. Mr. Johnson sat at the kitchen table in his blue work overalls. He had a big grin on his face.

"Come here Mandy. I've got something for you." Mandy walked over to Mr. Johnson. He reached down to a small basket by his feet and brought up a small puppy. "You seemed to be taking a shine to this young un so I thought you'd like to be her new mama." Mandy took the puppy and looked at her big brown eyes. Mr. Johnson was right. This was the puppy that she especially liked, the smallest one.

"Well, what do you say to Mr. Johnson, Mandy?"

"Huh?"

"Mr. Johnson just brought you a present. What do you say?"

"Thank you Mr. Johnson."

Mandy took her new puppy to her room, and lay down on the carpet with her. The puppy licked her cheek. Mandy smiled. She was so little, so little to be away from her mother. "It's nice here Puppy." The puppy whimpered. She wriggled free from her arms and began to sniff and search about the room. "What are you looking for, Puppy? Your mother? She's not here. She's in another place. Do you miss her?" Mandy watched and talked to the little puppy for a long time. She could hear Mama Rose cleaning and singing to the radio downstairs. Then she made up her mind. She scooped the puppy up in her arms and tiptoed downstairs.

She peeked around the corner. Mama Rose was vacuuming the living room. She decided to go out the back door through the kitchen. She had been to Mr. Johnson's farm many times. She was sure that she could remember the way. She clutched the puppy close to her and spoke gently to her. "It will be all right Puppy. Soon you'll be back with your mother."

The barn door
was open. Mandy
took her new little
charge over to the corner
of the barn where its mother and
brothers and sisters scampered in

the hay. "I'll miss you Puppy." Tears began to roll down Mandy's cheeks. She backed up slowly to the barn door, watching the puppy scramble over her siblings, trying to reach her mother.

"Whoa there, Mandy, what are you doing here so late?" Mr. Johnson gently caught Mandy's shoulder as she turned around. "I was just finishing milking the cows and thought I heard a voice in here. Does Mama Rose know you're here?"

Mandy shook her head as she looked up into Mr. Johnson's weathered face. He pushed his cap back and brushed his brow with the back of his arm. "Well now, it seems to me it must be something mighty important to bring you all the way over here close to dark." Just then the puppies whimpered, and Mr. Johnson looked in their direction, eyes narrowing in the dim light. Mandy's puppy continued to struggle in the midst of the brood. Taking Mandy by the hand, he set the milk bucket down on one side of a hay bale, and motioned for

Mandy to sit next to him on the other side. He nodded towards the puppies.

"I think your little one needs you, Mandy." Mandy hung her head. "Can you tell me why you brought the puppy back? Didn't you like her?" Mandy nodded. It was quiet for a long time. Big tears rolled down Mandy's cheek. Mr. Johnson pulled a handkerchief out of his overall pockets and handed it to her. "Mandy, you miss your mother, don't you?" Mandy nodded again. "And you thought the puppy would miss her Mommy too?" Again she nodded, and the tears began to roll some more. Mr. Johnson squeezed Mandy's shoulder gently. She leaned against him and cried. "That's okay, Mandy. I know you miss your Mommy. Do you know why you're with Mama Rose now?"

Mandy sniffled. "I know Miss Michaels said that Mommy couldn't take care of me. Doesn't she love me any more?"

"I think your mother loves you very much, Mandy, but she isn't well. That's why Miss Michaels put you with Mama Rose. She's your foster mother now. That means she will love you and take care of you while your mother tries to get well. Sometimes mothers or fathers can't give to their children all that they need even though they love them."

"Look at Taffy over there, lying so quiet. She's plumb tuckered out trying to feed all her babies, and some of them aren't getting enough milk, especially your little puppy. Set right there. I've got something for you." Reaching into his side pocket, he pulled out a rubber glove. He dipped it into the milk pail until the fingers bulged with frothy white milk. He tied a knot on the wrist end. Scooping up Mandy's little puppy, he placed it in her arms. Milk dribbled out as he pricked a hole in one of the glove fingers. Mandy held the glove as the puppy sucked eagerly.

Mandy looked up at Mr. Johnson. "I would like to take care of her. Do you think she'll love me?"

"I think she'll love you very much, just like Mama Rose loves you."

The puppy pulled her mouth away from the glove, milk dribbling down her chin. She closed her eyes, and nuzzled against Mandy's chest.

"I think I'll call her Sunny like the sunflowers in the field."

QUESTIONS AND ANSWERS TO GUIDE
DISCUSSION ABOUT FOSTER CARE

Mandy is living with Mama Rose, her "foster mother". What is a foster mother?

A foster mother or father is a person who has agreed to take care of a child who is in foster care. A foster parent has had training by the state to learn how to be a caring parent to a foster child.

What is foster care?

Foster care is the temporary placement of a child outside his or her own home so that the child will be in a safe, stable, and nurturing environment.

Why is a child placed in foster care?

There are many reasons that a child has to leave his or her own home and be placed in foster care. Every child needs to be loved, properly cared for, and safe. Sometimes the parents are unable to provide the necessary security and care.

How long does a foster child remain with a foster parent?

Foster children stay with a foster parent until their own parents are able to provide a safe and nurturing environment to their child. Sometimes this is a short time, and sometimes much longer.

Do foster children always return to their own parents?

No. Some parents are too sick or too incapable of ever taking care of their child properly. When this happens the foster child remains with their foster parent, or sometimes is adopted.

Who decides when a child must go into foster care?

In the story, the farmer mentions "Miss Michaels". She is a social worker, who works for the state. She helps the child move to the foster home and helps the foster parent get to know the child. She also works with the parents to see if they can in time provide the necessary safe, stable, caring home for their child.